Dragon Trouble

Penelope Lively

Illustrated by
VALERIE LITTLEWOOD

HEINEMANN · LONDON

William Heinemann Ltd
10 Upper Grosvenor Street, London W1X 9PA

LONDON · MELBOURNE · TORONTO
JOHANNESBURG · AUCKLAND

First published 1984, Reprinted 1985
Text © Penelope Lively 1984
Illustrations © Valerie Littlewood 1984

A school pack of BANANAS 1–6
is available from
Heinemann Educational Books
ISBN 0 435 00100 0

434 93022 9
Printed in Hong Kong by
Imago Publishing Ltd

THERE WERE DRAGONS in Cornwall,
once. Hundreds of years ago. Or maybe
thousands. It could be that there still
are, from time to time—just the odd one,
here and there. Anyway, this is what
happened to a boy of nine called Peter,
last summer.

He was spending the holidays with his
grandfather, in a small town somewhere
around the middle of Cornwall. It was an
ordinary little grey stone town with
houses and shops and a market

square – not the sort of place where you'd
expect to find unusual things happening.

Peter's grandfather, though, was
rather less ordinary. He lived by himself
in a splendidly untidy cottage with a
canary in a cage and two rabbits in a
hutch in the garden.

When Peter went to stay with him
they did whatever they both felt like and
had chips for every meal. Sometimes
they stayed in bed till lunch-time and
other days they played card-games all
day and once they decided to make a five
foot model aeroplane and sat up all night

doing it. I have to tell you that it all came unstuck the next day, but they both felt it had been worth it.

'Don't forget to buy Grandpa a card for his birthday,' Peter's mother had said. The day before the birthday, though, Peter decided that just a card would not do for such an excellent

grandfather. He went off by himself
into the town to look for a present: a
rather special present, it would have
to be.

Tobacco? No, that was dull.
Chocolates? A corkscrew with a handle
in the shape of an anchor? An ashtray
with a map of Cornwall on it? Nothing
he saw seemed right at all. He wandered
into the town square. It was market day

and there were fruit and vegetable stalls
and shirt and jeans stalls and stalls selling
dog food and bird seed, and a great many
people. There was also a junk stall at
which Peter stopped. This was more
promising. He thought about buying a
ship in a green glass bottle, but it was

much more than he could afford. An old
wind-up gramophone would have been
just the thing, but that was expensive
too.

Then he caught sight of one of those
glass domes on a stand that usually have
a couple of stuffed birds on a branch
under them. This one, though, had a
twiggy nest instead, and inside the nest
were two large reddish speckled eggs.

As soon as Peter saw it he knew that
this would be the perfect present. It
might not be what Grandpa had always
wanted, but he would want it as soon as

he saw it. And it was not too expensive; the glass was cracked and there were several chips out of the stand, so that it had been reduced to two pounds.

Peter bought it.

He was absolutely right: Grandpa was delighted. 'Now that's what I call a present,' he said. 'Original. Not your run-of-the-mill box of handkerchiefs or packet of pipe-cleaners. Just the thing for my mantelpiece.'

So the glass dome was put in the centre

of the mantelpiece, and that evening, since it was rather chilly, Grandpa lit a fire and he and Peter sat in front of it and ate fish and chips off their knees and admired Peter's present. 'Victorian, it'll be,' said Grandpa. 'A hundred years old or so, I'd reckon.'

It was Peter who came down first in the morning. He drew the curtains and had a look at the weather (raining) and then glanced across the room at the glass dome.

Underneath it, something was moving. He stood stock still and stared. Impossible! He moved closer.

The eggs had gone. In their place were two small lizard-like creatures scrabbling frantically at the glass. For a few moments Peter gazed in amazement. Then he rushed upstairs to fetch Grandpa.

Together they inspected the creatures more carefully. They were about five inches long. They had greenish scales blotched with red, legs with tiny claws, long tails with ends barbed like an arrow, and very small . . .

'Wings!' said Grandpa, putting on his glasses. 'Would you believe it! Wings— no two ways about it!'

The creatures continued to scrabble at the glass. 'What they look like,' said Peter, hardly daring to say it, 'is dragons.'

Grandpa nodded. 'You've put your finger on it. What we've got here, to my mind, is a pair of young dragons. Extraordinary! It'll be the heat of the fire that did it. Those eggs must have been laid away in some cold attic all these years. Bring them into the warm and they hatch. It's a wonderful thing, Nature.'

Clearly, they could not leave the dragons where they were. Apart from anything else, there would not be enough air for them under the glass.

Grandpa found an old cardboard box
which they lined with newspaper. Very
carefully they lifted the glass dome from
its base and tipped the creatures into it.

'Question is,' said Grandpa, 'what do
we feed them on?'

This turned out to be a problem. They
tried breadcrumbs, bird food, Kit-E-Kat,
banana and lettuce, all of which the

dragons ignored. They retreated to the end of the box and sat there forlornly. It wasn't until Grandpa and Peter had their lunch, which was fish fingers and chips, that they perked up. They began to sniff and scratch at the sides of the box. Peter chopped up a piece of fish finger and offered it to the dragons. They fell on it happily.

The dragons flourished. After a week or so they were getting too big for the

box. Grandpa repaired an old rabbit
hutch and they moved them out into the
garden and put them in that. They ate a
packet of fish fingers every day, with a
tin of salmon as an occasional treat.
Nothing else would they touch, except
prawns, which they ate whole, whiskers
and all.

Peter and Grandpa were extremely
proud of them. 'You can keep your
budgies and your cats and your dogs,'
said Grandpa. 'I like an unusual pet. And
these beat everything, eh?'

The dragons, admittedly, were not
especially cosy pets. They did not care

for being stroked and were inclined to
hiss when disturbed. But they were very
handsome. Their scales were now a rich
grass-green decorated with
reddish-brown spots. They had fine
crests along their necks and their tails
swished and curled. Their wings were
transparent and large enough now to
flap. They would sit in their hutch
preening and flapping and nibbling at
fish fingers.

Given all this, I suppose what came next was inevitable. Grandpa decided to exhibit the dragons at the town's annual Pet Show.

They attracted immediate attention. And caused instant trouble. 'What are they, for heaven's sake?' exclaimed the lady in charge of arranging entries.

'Well,' said Grandpa, 'you've got a point there. I can see they don't fit in with Dogs or Cats or Cage-birds. Reptiles, maybe?'

Eventually, after a great deal of talk among the judges, the dragons were entered in the Miscellaneous Class, along with some tortoises, a tank of newts, two parrots and a grass-snake.

They had a great success. People crowded round their hutch peering through the wire-netting at them and exclaiming. The dragons appeared to

enjoy the attention; they strutted up and
down and played together. They were
now almost the size of rabbits.

The trouble started when it came to
the judging. Two of the three judges
wanted to give them First Prize but the
third objected strongly, on the grounds
that nobody knew what to call them.
Finally a vote was taken. The dragons

were given a red rosette, which Grandpa
pinned proudly to the hutch.

The awkward judge, a stout woman
whose poodle had failed to win a prize in
the Dog Class, remarked loudly that the
things looked to her like something that
ought to be in a museum and she
wouldn't be surprised if they carried
nasty diseases. She tapped the hutch
with her umbrella and then sprang
backwards with a shriek. There was a
sizzling sound and a smell of scorching.

The dragons had learned to spit
flames. Very small flames, mind you,

but flames all the same. Grandpa and Peter took them home hurriedly, before people could ask any more questions or make any more comments than they already were. On the way Grandpa bought a fire extinguisher.

'Just in case. They were provoked, mind. I reckon they'll settle down again once we get them back.' He spoke severely to the dragons, who looked now as though butter wouldn't melt in their mouths.

There was a short piece about them in
the paper, headed LOCAL
PENSIONER'S MYSTERY PETS.
Grandpa had mixed feelings about this;
he thought the photograph of himself
unflattering and he was worried that it
would arouse too much curiosity.

'There's no limit to how nosy people can be, you take my word for it. Jealous, too. That's what was up with that woman. Plain jealous. Her with her poodle done up like a lamb chop. Next thing, we'll have everyone wanting what we've got. And I'm not breeding them. I've had enough trouble that way with rabbits.'

He was right to be worried, as it turned out. Three days later there was a knock at the door and on the step stood a man in uniform who said he was the Pest Control Officer and he had reason to believe that there were some unusual animals in the house. Grandpa and Peter stared at him in alarm.

'Lizards of some sort, is it?' continued the Pest Control Officer. 'The name's George, by the way.' He held out a printed card to Grandpa. 'Mr George. Won't take a minute, but it's my job to check up. All right if I come in?'

They let him in and took him through to the garden. There was nothing else, really, they could do. Mr George squatted down in front of the hutch and studied the dragons. There was a silence.

'Ah,' said Mr George. 'Yes. I see. A pair of . . . um . . . A pair of those things.'

There was a glint, now, in Grandpa's eye. 'What,' he said, 'counts as pests?'

Mr George stood up. 'Rats. Mice.

22

Cockroaches. Black beetles. Wasps.'

'And are what we've got in that hutch any of those?' continued Grandpa.

'Strictly speaking,' said Mr George, 'no.'

'Then,' said Grandpa triumphantly, 'what's wrong with us keeping them?'

Mr George considered. 'Strictly speaking,' he said again, 'nothing.' He cast a doubtful look down at the dragons. 'But they're a bit out of the way, you must admit. What . . . um . . . what exactly would you call them now?'

'Dragons,' said Peter, before he could help himself.

Mr George laughed. He patted Peter on the head. 'Got quite an imagination, your grandson, hasn't he?' he said to Grandpa. 'Well, we'll leave it at that for now. But I'll have to make a report on it. And mind you keep them under control – they look to me as though they could give you a nasty nip.'

As soon as he had gone Peter and Grandpa heaved sighs of relief. It had been a dangerous moment, they agreed. 'Someone's been tittle-tattling,' said Grandpa darkly. 'Her with the poodle, I daresay. Or one of the nosy-parkers in this street. Best thing we can do is lie low. Else . . .'

'Else we mightn't be able to keep them?' said Peter anxiously.

Grandpa nodded.

But there was worse to come. A couple of days later Peter went out in the

evening to feed the dragons and found to
his horror that the hutch was empty.
Part of the wire-netting front had been

ripped away, evidently by strong little
dragon claws. He and Grandpa searched
the garden; there was no sign of them.
They remembered with alarm that lately
the dragons had been flapping their
wings more and more, like fledglings
about to take off. Had they flown right

away? Grandpa shook his head sadly. 'I don't know as how they'd fend for themselves in that case. How're they going to get across to folk that what they fancy is fish fingers and nothing else?'

'Or tinned salmon,' added Peter.

They searched the house, just in case, and then came outside again. And then, both at once, they noticed a curious noise coming from the next door garden. A sound of splashing.

'What's Mrs Hammond up to?' said Grandpa, frowning. Mrs Hammond was the next door neighbour.

'But she's away!' Peter exclaimed. 'Don't you remember – she asked us to water her tomatoes for her.'

They dashed to the fence and looked over. In the middle of Mrs Hammond's garden was her most treasured possession, a large pond covered with water-lilies and bullrushes amid which swam a couple of dozen fat goldfish.

And there at the edge of the pond was one of the dragons, contentedly munching a goldfish that it held in its

front claws. Even as they watched, the
second one rose from a clump of rushes,
whooshed up into the air with an untidy

flapping of wings and plunged straight
down into the pond. A few seconds later
it rose to the surface, scrambled out,

shook itself like a dog and settled down to eat the goldfish that it, too, was now clutching.

'She's going to be *furious*!' cried Peter.

Grandpa was already rushing into the house. He came out with a piece of green nylon garden netting and a bucket. 'Quick! Over that fence!'

Peter scrambled over and set about the difficult business of catching the dragons. Grandpa watched anxiously from the other side and shouted words of advice. The dragons scuttled round the pond hissing angrily and sometimes spitting a few feeble flames. From time to time they took off and flapped a few yards across Mrs Hammond's lawn before flopping to the ground. Evidently they weren't yet very good at flying. At last Peter managed to net them both and get them into the bucket, which he passed over the fence to Grandpa. There were only three goldfish left in the pond.

They put the dragons back in the hutch, where they huddled into the corner still hissing quietly. Peter and Grandpa hurried off to the pet shop in

the High Street and they bought the
entire stock of goldfish.

'Think she'll notice the difference?'
asked Peter when he had emptied them
into Mrs Hammond's pond.

Grandpa shook his head. 'I doubt if a person gets what you might call close to a fish.'

That evening they took a long hard look at the situation. Things could not go on like this.

'You know something?' said Grandpa. 'I think I know what it is we've got out there. What we've got is a pair of sea-dragons. Fish-eaters, see? I should have cottoned on to it before.'

'Do you think they're full-size yet?' asked Peter.

Grandpa shrugged. 'Maybe, maybe not. But one thing I'm clear about; they're getting out of hand. They're not the sort of thing you can keep in your back garden for ever.'

The more they thought about it the more it seemed to them that there were only two things they could do. They could give the dragons to a zoo. Or they could let them go.

'They'd hate it in a zoo,' said Peter. 'Being stared at all the time. And fed peanuts. But where could we let them go?'

'Where they ought to be,' said Grandpa. 'Their natural habitat. The sea.'

And so the great idea was born. It took a lot of planning. They would have to take the dragons to the coast on the bus, since Grandpa did not have a car. Then they would have to find a beach with rocky cliffs from which to launch the dragons.

They borrowed a cat basket from a neighbour (Grandpa spun a story about having to take his rabbits to the vet), got the dragons into it, with some difficulty, and set off. The bus journey was tricky; the dragons scrabbled around in the basket throughout so that Grandpa and Peter had to talk loudly to drown the noise. But at last they reached the coast and set off for a beach where Grandpa knew there were cliffs dropping down into the sea.

There were a good number of people on the beach at the foot of the cliffs. Grandpa and Peter stood at the top of the path that led down there and watched for a few minutes.

'Be all right so long as we can get them off good and quick,' said Grandpa. 'Straight out to sea and no nonsense.'

They opened the cat basket. Peter pushed it nearer to the edge of the cliff. The dragons stuck their heads out and flapped their wings. They climbed onto the edge of the basket and flapped more busily.

'That's it,' said Peter. 'Shoo! Go on – fly!'

And the dragons took off. They soared upwards and then . . . oh, horrors! . . . they began to sink slowly towards the beach. They spun and flapped and fluttered down at last upon the sand. Peter and Grandpa gave one look, and set off at once helter-skelter down the steep path to the beach.

They got to the spot at which the
dragons had landed and began to search
for them. People were sitting around
having picnics or sunbathing or reading
newspapers. There was no sign of the
dragons. Suddenly Peter caught sight of

one of them. It was sitting beside
someone's picnic basket contentedly
munching a fish paste sandwich. And the
other one was stretched out on the
ramparts of some children's sandcastle,
sunning itself.

Peter rushed forward to grab them at
the same moment as the owner of the
fish paste sandwich turned round and
gave a cry of alarm. 'Excuse me!' Peter
panted. 'My dog . . .' He snatched up the
dragon just as the man was reaching for
his spectacles. He seized the other one
and popped them both into the cat
basket, which Grandpa was holding out.

Several people were now staring at them and muttering. They made for the cliff path, hastily.

At the top Grandpa said grimly, 'One more try. Or it's the zoo for the pair of them. We've done our level best.'

A breeze had sprung up. Perhaps that helped, or perhaps the dragons had simply got better at flying after a little practice. Anyway, this time they soared upwards and stayed up, floating and flapping over the beach and the people and out over the water. 'That's the spirit!' cried Grandpa. Peter clapped and waved.

The dragons whisked their tails and swooped in circles. Their scales caught the sun and glittered until after a few minutes all Peter and Grandpa could see was two twinkling spots of light. And as they watched the two spots plunged down suddenly into the sea, and then sprang up out of it again in a gleaming shower, and then down and up again . . .

'They're fishing!' cried Peter. And he and Grandpa turned away and began to walk slowly back to the road to catch the bus.

Maybe those were the last dragons in Cornwall. Maybe not. There's no telling. As Grandpa said, it's a wonderful thing, Nature.